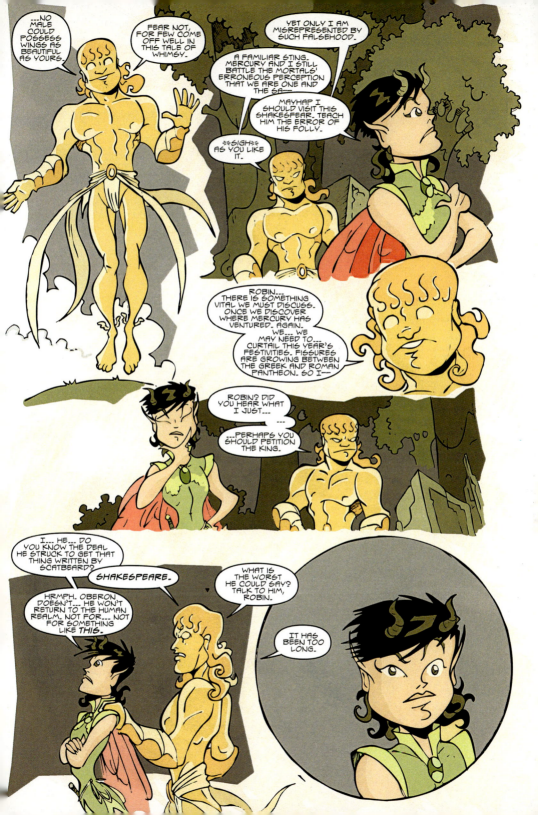

SPEAK.

BE BRIEF.

I... IT'S ABOUT...

—THAT PITIFUL 'PLAY' WHICH MAKES ME VICTIM TO CHILDISH MAGIC, AKIN TO SOME SHAMBLING NEOPHYTE?

THE PROUD FAIRY QUEEN, FAWNING OVER USELESS MORTALS? HM?

IF ONLY YOU TRULY KNEW WHAT IT IS TO BE A WOMAN IN THIS REALM.

WE ARE THE FACES OF FAERIE. ESPECIALLY IN THE SNATCHES OF THE MORTALS' LIMITED EXPERIENCE.

WE ARE THEIR FANTASY.

YET, THEY BETHINK US SUBSERVIENT. PETTY. MOTLEY MINDED PLAYTHINGS.

TITANIA, I DON'T—

QUIET, CHILD.

What if you had the chance to get away from your life? To be the hero of your very own myth? To have your tales of adventure told across generations, long after you're gone? At the risk of constant danger?

Would you take that chance?

Eve did. But the path to glory comes with unforeseen and life-changing consequences.

*Magic of Myths* chronicles her journey – a broken soul trapped within a world which is bizarre, dangerous, and somewhat… familiar.

Magical armour, a myriad of monsters, a mysterious benefactor and five life-threatening labours… welcome to a place where the power of imagination and mass belief is everything.

But what if fantasy…

…is the only reality you have?

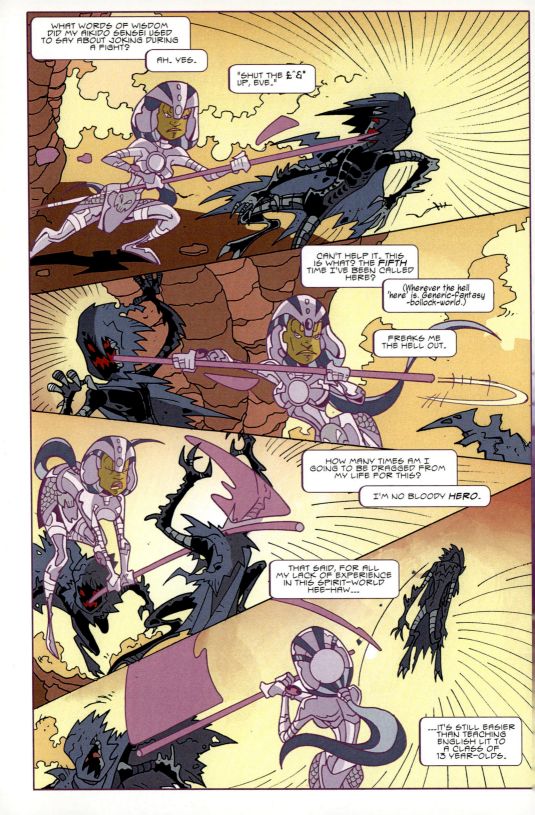

# *Magic of Myths: Faerie*
## behind the scenes script

This behind the scenes script nearly didn't make it into the book.

True, we've built a little tradition with **Magic of Myths** in that we detail the script and a 'making of' commentary whenever we release a book (apologies to those who missed it if you didn't get the Special Edition of Season two). But *Magic of Myths: Faerie* is a little different. Given its strong roots in *A Midsummer Night's Dream*, it made sense to leave parts of the story entirely up to interpretation, true to Shakespeare's original plays. Faerie has a lot of metatextual narrative, as well as hidden facets that are best left for the reader to discover – and we wouldn't want to ruin your fun in finding them.

But at the same time, our fanbase seems to really like seeing a glimpse behind the curtain of our series. And given the relatively unusual aspect of this book – using Shakespeare and his various literary devices – is something rarely explored in comics, it seemed like a missed opportunity not to include something which scrutinised its workings.

So, a compromise. What you're about to read is the original 'drawing script' to *Magic of Myths: Faerie*, pre final edits. This "warts 'n all" version is about 95% of what ended up in the final story, with that remaining 5% consisting of error corrections, new parts or revisions which came up during email conversations between myself and Sergio, minor changes for clarity after I saw the artwork, and so on.

At the same time, we're not providing a commentary this time (aside from this intro, obviously). We're leaving you to pick up on any nuances, our thoughts behind certain creative decisions and things left unsaid which have emerged in the text or artwork. At the very least we can tell you that there are references – visual and dialogue based – to some of Shakespeare's other plays, nods to things which have happened in seasons one and two of **Magic of Myths** and clues to forthcoming events in the series... all mixed in with iambic/trochaic pentameters, rhyming couplets, language tricks, a reference to medieval French poetry and other buried nuggets.

And – as with every season of **Magic of Myths** so far – there's also a hint as how this is all going to end...

# Magic of Myths: Faerie

by Corey Brotherson

## Page 1 – six panels

*Panel one*

To kick things off, we're going to have a page which is written in rhyming couplets in a mixture of iambic and trochaic pentameter, which details the history of how and why Robin, Mercury and Hermes meet up, and then do so every year. It's a one page montage, so feel free to give it whatever style or feel you want to keep it visually interesting, using the panel borders and gutters however you see fit. The only thing to potentially avoid is a 'ye olde storybook sketch style' (like you did for the V and Byron novella) as we may need that later on in the story where it may be more suitable. But the main things here to capture is a sense of this happening a long time ago (so you can change their hairstyles/clothing each time shift) and not in the 'present' of the story (which is still in *Magic of Myths*' past). Hopefully that all makes sense?

Right, so panel one! This a panel where we're introduced to the concept of what will follow - three tricksters meeting. For this, we'll see their three symbols - the symbol of the forest (so maybe a tree and leaf, but I'm open to suggestions) for the faeries, the symbol of Hermes' staff and Mercury's symbol - place Robin's symbol in the middle of the two others, and if possible, give Mercury and Hermes' symbols a similiar style to donate them being brothers/of the same ilk - one of the problems we'll need to show is that while Hermes and Mercury are the same in established mythology, our story has them as two beings, so if we can show that visually throughout (almost twins in a way, but distinct enough, as you have in your sketches) that would be great.

> NARRATOR CAPTION [Shakespearian pamphlet style, curled edges, ornate]: Know the truest lies lay deep in tale,
> Slight and rare insight behind a veil.

*Panel two*

In Greenie's forest, lush and full of life. The three of them stand. Robin has her eyes narrowed and slightly suspicious, arms crossed, while Hermes is smiling and Mercury stands stoic with his caduceus but there's a slight Flash style blur to him whenever he's present, as if he's always moving. A note here as to their relationship which will be shown visually through the story - Hermes will fall in love with Robin, Robin will be oblivious and fancy Mercury and Mercury is aware of both but does not act (as to not hurt either of them). As this page goes on, you can show this subtly, before we get into the 'present'. If you're using colour, Robin's wings are a cautious dark yellow.

> NARRATOR CAPTION [Shakespearian pamphlet style, curled edges, ornate]: Here it started, fair from foul and jest,
> Friendly japes as proof whom may be best.

*Panel three*
Another time now, as Hermes has become the butt of one of their jokes - he has an ass's head (as reference to *A Midsummer Night's Dream*). Robin is beside herself laughing, unable to stand, while Mercury smiles ruefully, one of his hands half-face palming himself. If you're using colour, Robin's wings are bright, happy colours, a rainbow mixture of yellow, blue, green, red and orange. There is a sign hammered into the grass, saying in handwritten paint:

> Rules:
> 1) Tricks yay
> 2) Lies nay
> 3) Always obey 1) and 2)

> And it's signed at the bottom in their individual handwriting:
> Robin, Hermes and Mercury

> NARRATOR CAPTION [Shakespearian pamphlet style, curled edges, ornate]: Mighty tricksters matching wit and guile, Treats joined tricks, fun tests of guts and wile.

*Panel four*
Another year now, in Greenie's forest (in autumn) as all three are sitting having a picnic. Hermes is smiling and laughing with Robin, but while Robin is doing the same, she's glancing at Mercury who is chatting with Greenie (who is above them - although we only ever see his leafy face, which can be anywhere near the larger trees of his wood). If you're using colour, Robin's wings are a happy bright sunshine yellow, tinged with pink.

> NARRATOR CAPTION [Shakespearian pamphlet style, curled edges, ornate]: Bonded three of Greek, Roman, and Fairie, Friends of farce with plot to convene yearly.

*Panel five - six*
Same as last panel, but between these two panels here we're drifting away from the scene, up into the sky, which will act as our transition to the next scene/page. As we get further, the panels can get a little darker.

> NARRATOR CAPTION [Shakespearian pamphlet style, curled edges, ornate]: Yet through time, our dearest joys will bend: All false and good things must depart to an...

## Page 2 – six panels

*Panel one*
A dash of lightning streaks across the dark sky. An ominous opening to go with the hyperbolic dialogue. A lovely but dark coloured fairy style butterfly darts through the sky, with what looks like eyes on its wings (both eyes and wings are big themes and symbols in this story). We'll be following it down the page, so feel free to make it travel across panels and the gutters if you want. This butterfly represents freedom in literally a dark and stormy time, seemingly unaware of the danger it's in – very much our metaphor for Robin and her plight in the story. We're in the 'present', now.

> CAPTION [no boxout]: Faerie, 1596
> ROBIN [off panel, shouting]: I HATE THEE, BILLIAM SKAKEBEER!

*Panel two*
We pan down a little from the sky to reveal a forest full of trees. Beautiful, but almost cowering in the presence of growing storm. It's not yet raining. The butterfly flutters down the page, further.

>HERMES [off panel]: Please, Robin, this rage ill becomes you.
>HERMES [off panel, small]: And I believe 'tis 'William Shakespeare'...
>ROBIN [off panel]: I hate him, and he's a [swear symbols]!

*Panel three*
We see the main scene at last. Standing at ground level is Hermes, who is looking slightly apologetic and trying to appeal to Robin (who has her dagger/knife attached to her belt), who is flapping her (bright, angry red) wings and hovering off the ground. She's shaking a parchment manuscript with anger, we can see the title 'A Midsummer Night's Dream' on the cover. Hermes is in love with Robin, but she never notices – so their body language should reflect this. Our butterfly is exiting the scene, unnoticed by the two.

>HERMES: Calm, gentle Robin, calm.
>ROBIN: Have you read it, Hermes? This... this... **thing?**
>ROBIN [small/quiet]: No doubt being duplicated across the realm like a plague. Arrogant North wood fairies...

*Panel four*
A close up of Robin, who is still looking cute but angry. She holds up the pages of the play (Act II, Scene I, which we'll see closer in a bit) pointing a finger at the lines.

>ROBIN: "Ho ho ho"? "Hobgoblin"? "Merry wanderer of the night"?!?
>ROBIN [small]: Although I admit to liking this "Lord, what fools these mortals be" part. Appropriate.
>ROBIN: But look!

*Panel five*
We see a page of the play, Robin points her finger at the following line on a page which says:

>Fairy:
>*Either I mistake your shape and making quite,*
>*Or else you are that shrewd and knavish sprite*
>*Call'd Robin Goodfellow: are not you he*

>ROBIN [off panel]: "He"? "**Goodfellow**"?!?

*Panel six*
Robin stands proud, spreading her beautiful, bold red wings wide.

>ROBIN: I am no "good*fellow*".
>HERMES [off panel]: 'Tis true...

**Page 3 – six panels**

*Panel one*
Hermes smiles, charming and sweet. He's trying to disarm Robin with his words.

>HERMES: ...no male could possess wings as beautiful as yours.
>HERMES: Fear not, for few come off well in this tale of whimsy.

*Panel two*
Both of them in panel. Robin staring up into the sky, thinking about loud as she cradles her chin. Hermes starts to look exhausted.

>ROBIN: Yet only I am misrepresented by such falsehood.
>HERMES: A familiar sting. Mercury and I still battle the mortals' erroneous perception that we are one and the sa--
>ROBIN [overlapping]: Mayhap I should visit this Shakesfear. Teach him the error of his folly.
>HERMES: [Sighs] As you like it.

*Panel three*
Hermes looks sad and serious now.

>HERMES: Robin...there is something vital we must discuss. Once we discover where Mercury has ventured. Again.
>HERMES: We... we may need to... curtail this year's festivities. Fissures are growing between the Greek and Roman pantheon. So I--

*Panel four*
Robin is looking stern, lost in thought. She's not taking his words in. Hermes looks morose, realising – not for the first time – that the woman he loves is not listening to him (not intentionally, more from a lack of awareness which Robin suffers from).

>HERMES: Robin? Did you hear what I just...
>HERMES: ...
>HERMES: ...perhaps you should petition the king.

*Panel five*
Closer in. Hermes gently puts a hand on Robin's shoulder, Robin still has her back to him, thinking.

>ROBIN: I... he... do you know the deal he struck to get that thing written by Scatbeard?
>HERMES: Shakespeare.
>ROBIN: Hrmph. Oberon doesn't... he won't return to the human realm. Not for... not for something like this.
>HERMES: What is the worst he could say? Talk to him, Robin.

*Panel six*
A close up of Robin, raising an eyebrow in trepidation, her features softening for the first time as she takes in Hermes' words.

>HERMES [off panel]: It has been too long.

## Page 4 – five panels

*Panel one*
Robin flies along the woods, wings more mixing red with a slightly nervous blue, as they will remain for this scene – four of Oberon's guards, dressed in full battle garb and armed with swords and spears watch her suspiciously as they walk. Robin is oblivious, clutching the script in her hands, as she'll hold his (firmly) through the next two scenes.

>NO DIALOGUE

*Panel two*
We look closer at the guards as we see the back of Robin as she flies past. One of the guards has raised his spear, but another guard has his hand on it gentling pushing it back down as to say "no, we are not aggressive

towards her – let her carry on". They both look stern, battle fierce in their expression.

GUARD: No. Not now. Remember the terms.

*Panel three*
Robin has landed and walks towards the gates of the large faerie palace. Two guards stand on the side of the gate, but do not look at her.

NO DIALOGUE

*Panel four*
Inside the throne room of the palace now, we see two swords clash in front of us (we can't see who holds them, just the swords creating an X shape, sparks flying - this is a visual callback to Season 2 of *Magic of Myths*, the war between Romans and Greeks). We can see Robin the background, looking slightly shocked as she's come through the doors. If you can, have her framed by the swords, so she's 'standing' in the middle of the two swords clashing.

ROBIN: ...Oberon?

*Panel five*
From closer (and behind) Robin, we see a wider view of the throne room, which has been converted into a makeshift training room. There are two thrones – one is immaculate, the other is carved and chipped (as if it's been attacked), holding various weapons. In the centre of the room, Oberon is sparing with a long sword against two guards (also wielding swords). None of them wear armour, but the guards are sweating. All three look stern and in the moment as they stand off each other, sizing each other up.

ROBIN: A word?

**Page 5 – six panels**

*Panel one*
The three clash as Robin watches. Oberon ducks a sword swung at his head by one guard as he blocks the other guard's sword downwards (he holds the hilt high and the blade down).

OBERON: No.

*Panel two*
Oberon suddenly flash kicks (kinda like Guile from *Street Fighter 2*, but far more elegantly) the guard in front of him, while still holding his sword. The other guard is shocked at what he sees, while the guard being kicked is caught on the chin and knocked backwards.

OBERON: No.

*Panel three*
Still in the air, Oberon (with both hands on the hilt of his blade) thrusts his sword towards the standing guard who barely blocks the attack. The kicked guard is on the floor, on his back.

OBERON: **NO.**

*Panel four*
Oberon becomes a slight magic-tinged blur as he does kicks the guard in the head, while still in the air, also cutting some of the guard's hair from a sword swipe.

OBERON: Disappointing. Extremely disappointing.

*Panel five*
Oberon lands, his two guards both laid out from the blows, but conscious. He has his back to us and Robin looks worried.

> OBERON: Again. Better.
> OBERON: As **men**.
> ROBIN [off panel]: ...Oberon?

*Panel six*
Close up. Oberon turns his head, barely glancing sideways at his daughter, almost pretending he didn't hear, but his emotion is clear: it's a vicious look of disgust.

> OBERON: **LEAVE.**

## Page 6 – five panels

*Panel one*
New scene. Robin, wings even more blue than red now (with a little green - she's even more nervous to the point of near sickness) stands outside of a large and extravagant (bejewelled and golden) double doors with no handle, holding the script (which is scrunched and wrinkled in her grip). They dwarf her. Although we can't see Robin's expression, her body language suggests she's nervous (maybe hugging herself?). This is the entrance to Titania's magical domain, so it oozes a sense of power and mystery – much like Oberon's scene was all about physicality, this is another display of power.

> NO DIALOGUE

*Panel two*
A close up of Robin, we see, nervously unsure of what she wants to do here. There's a genuine fear – she's about to meet her mother and that frightens her, even more than her father.

> NO DIALOGUE

*Panel three*
From inside, the doors (it's dark) we see Robin anxiously enter. She's looking up and slightly to her side, unsure of what to expect in this place.

> NO DIALOGUE

*Panel four*
Blackness. Pure darkness as the doors close.

> ROBIN [in slight fright]: Oh!
> ROBIN [quietly/small]: ...oh...

*Panel five*
Same sized panel as *Panel four*. Robin's wings give off a slight light to illuminate her. Robin uses her free hand to hold her nose, from the smell of Titania's magic. It's an eerie scene, with Robin looking scared but is pushing on.

> ROBIN [quietly/small]: Ugh... pungent...
> ROBIN [quietly/small]: ...Titania...? Where are... hgf... that terrible arom...
> TITANIA [off panel]: **Silence.**

*Panel one*
We see Robin in the background, her puny light illuminating her as she holds her nose. In the foreground we see Titania's finely manicured hands, sparking with stars and magic, as she moulds what seems to be a head made of clay, which is outlined with red energy and giving off some sort of strange mist/gas. It had no features, no eyes, but it had a strong jawline. The light comes from Titania's magic. We don't see Titania as such, just her hands moulding (and if needed, part of her body) – we won't see her head/face until later, as we're building a sense of dread.

NO DIALOGUE

*Panel two*
Same as last panel but now Titania is carving the shape of an eye socket with her nail. With her other hand, she opens her palm as to say "now you can speak" (without turning to address Robin). Robin, in the background, looks fragile.

TITANIA: Speak.
TITANIA: Be brief.

*Panel three*
A close up of Robin, whose light barely illuminates her scared face. She looks slightly worried.

ROBIN: I... it's about...
TITANIA [off panel]: --that pitiful 'play' which make me victim to childish magic, akin to some shambling neophyte?
TITANIA [off panel]: The proud fairy queen, fawning over useless mortals? Hm?

*Panel four*
Same as last panel, but Robin looks even more worried.

TITANIA [off panel]: If only you truly knew what it is to be a woman in this realm.
TITANIA [off panel]: We are the faces of Faerie. Especially in the snatches of the mortals' **limited** experience.

*Panel five*
Back to Titania's carving, which she is now creating more features – still no eyes, but hollow eye sockets – but she's carving a mouth with long, jagged teeth. Nasty and haunting.

TITANIA: We are their fantasy.
TITANIA: Yet, they bethink us subservient. Petty. Motley minded playthings.

*Panel six*
Robin now, looking shocked and petrified at being shouted at.

ROBIN: Titania, I don't--
TITANIA [off panel, interrupting]: **QUIET, CHILD.**

## Page 8 – six panels

*Panel one*
Back to Titania's carving, and she sparks magic into the eyes of what looks like a perverted version of a female fairy – sinister and nightmarish, but still fairy-looking/features. The eyes are red and scary.

TITANIA: That, my dear "Puck", is the problem.
TITANIA: You are blind.

*Panel two*
We see Titania's hands with energy like lightening sparking between both palms, creating more light. We'll scroll up to her face for the first time in the next panel.

TITANIA: Our reality is controlled. By those who wish to possess the power mortal fantasy holds.

*Panel three*
We finally see Titania's face – smiling cruelly, beautiful and powerful, but very intimidating, especially in the glow of her magic.

TITANIA: Power which rightfully belongs to the women of Faerie.

*Panel four*
By contrast, we go back to Robin, who looks small and timid, in the weak light of her own magic.

TITANIA [off panel]: There is no place for those who has't not the **blood** to take it.
TITANIA [off panel]: Behold thyself. You come to **me** with your **pathetic** braying.

*Panel five*
Titania, who for the first time, glances to her side, as if to address Robin (not entirely). We see Robin in the background. Titania narrows her eyes, clearly unhappy.

TITANIA: You continuously and flagrantly break my law by **refusing** to wear **glamour**. And you use your gifts with hollow abandon.
TITANIA: Even those majestic wings are wasted.

*Panel six*
Back to Robin – who is starting to look slightly more put out now, a glimmer of anger starting to overtake her upset.

TITANIA [off panel]: You have the freedom of this realm. And what do you do with it?

### Page 9 – five panels

*Panel one*
Titania turns back to her horrific creation, which is starting to seem more alive and less like clay. She looks occupied and back to ignoring Robin.

TITANIA: You came for my counsel, little one, so leave with this:
TITANIA: Consider yourself grateful. For this abomination of what passes for a mortal script at least makes some use...

*Panel two*
Robin now, bearing teeth with anger.

TITANIA [off panel]: ...out of the disappointing waste that is your existence.

*Panel three*
From Robin's waist we see her clutch on to the handle of her dagger, shaking with anger.

NO DIALOGUE

*Panel four*
We see Robin's expression, which now looks sad – she realises that these words, as hurtful as they are, are true.

NO DIALOGUE

*Panel five*
She walks away towards the now opening door, her head slightly turned to look back. She's dejected and melancholic.

NO DIALOGUE

## Page 10 – six panels

*Panel one*
Robin walks away towards the now opening door, her head slightly turned to look back. She's dejected and melancholic. Her wings are now blue. She holds the script tightly in one hand.

NO DIALOGUE

*Panel two to three*
From over her shoulder (or however you feel it may be better), she stands outside of the large gates of the large faerie palace, looking at the script. The page says:

And then I will her charmed eye release
From monster's view, and all things shall be peace.

VOICE [no tail, telepathic, hollow]: Robin?

*Panel four*
Robin looks concerned, lifting her head up.

ROBIN: Poor timing, Greenie, I am--
VOICE [no tail, telepathic, hollow, interrupting]: Mercury, Hermes and I request thy presence at mine wood. 'Tis of grave importance.

*Panel five*
Robin smiles slightly at the news.

ROBIN: Mercury...!
VOICE [no tail, telepathic, grizzled, interrupting]: With **haste**, Robin.

*Panel six*
Scene changeover, as Robin (wings light orange, for nerves) flies into Greenie's wood, where Flash-like Mercury (with cadeaus staff) and Hermes are having an intense discussion. Greenie is over them, looking stern. Robin has the script tucked into her belt so her hands are free.

MERCURY: --and wasting time is not our domain.
ROBIN [interrupting]: What in [swear symbols]'s name is this?

## Page 11 – six panels

*Panel one*
Mercury tries to explain - he looks serious, but slightly worried. Robin interrupts, looking distressed but stern holding her palms up as to say "stop, hold it right there."

MERCURY: Ah, Robin, please excuse our brevity, we must forgo our usual festivities. Farewe--

ROBIN: Please, patience. I've had very little grace from supposed royalty today; I at least hope it from my friends.

*Panel two*
Close up of Greenie, who is looking concerned.

GREENIE [hollow]: I urged milady to come. This affects her directly.

*Panel three*
Mercury looks at the sad looking Hermes. Neither of them want this - Mercury wanted a swift exit and to spare his brother, Hermes hasn't chance to tell Robin how he feels.

NO DIALOGUE

*Panel four*
Mercury starts to explain.

MERCURY: Very well.
MERCURY: Faerie is becoming... **difficult** for outsiders such as my brother and I. We should not dally here.

*Panel five*
Robin looks slightly panicked and confused.

ROBIN: I don't understand, what has changed since...

*Panel six*
Same as last panel, but Robin is sniffing the air, trying to recognise the smell in the air.

ROBIN: ...since...
ROBIN: ...what... what is that strange scent?

### Page 12 – six panels

*Panel one*
Mercury looks confused.

MERCURY: What? What scent?

*Panel two*
Close up of Robin as the realisation hits, her eyes wide.

ROBIN: ...*Titania*.
ROBIN: You and... **that** was where you were?

*Panel three*
Mercury has been caught red-handed, and he's now on the back foot, trying to get out of this by blurting out the news. Hermes looks at his brother with shock.

MERCURY: I...
MERCURY: ...this is not the time to focus on dalliance, Robin! You are at **war**, for Hades' sake!
HERMES [small]: War..?

*Panel four*
Robin is stunned. She never saw it coming and this, and the news that Mercury is sleeping with (or at least seeing) her mother is a total surprise.

ROBIN: What?
ROBIN: ...No... I...

*Panel five*
Same as last, as a dark realisation hits her. This is truly a gut punch, and now it's dawning.

> ROBIN [small]: ...I... we're...
> ROBIN [small, to herself]: ... of course we are. Foolish, foolish little sprite.

*Panel six*
Mercury again, explaining as gently as he can. He's not angry, and realises what this means for them all.

> MERCURY: Your king and queen have agreed civil terms. Preparation before conflict. Soon your borders will close, trapping all inside. Outsiders within this kingdom will be conscripted, along with everyone else.
> MERCURY: Do you understand what I am saying?

### Page 13 – six panels

*Panel one*
Robin looks broken. Her wings have turned a pale, blue colour. She mumbles to herself.

> ROBIN [small]: She was right. They both were.
> HERMES [off panel]: Robin--

*Panel two*
Hermes extends an arm towards Robin, who is still trying to process this. Greenie looms over them.

> HERMES: --Come with us.
> MERCURY: Brother, our realms are hardly stable--
> GREENIE [hollow]: No. Milady cannot.

*Panel three*
Greenie explains, sadly.

> GREENIE [hollow]: I can feeleth her grace's spell already. Natives of Faerie art trapped hither, to battle. Those already absent wilt be magically drawn back. To prevent deserters.
> GREENIE [hollow]: I think... even my magik struggles to avert its effects.

*Panel four*
Mercury puts his hand on Hermes' shoulder.

> MERCURY: We must depart, lest we lose the time given as courtesy--

*Panel five*
Robin explodes in anger, flying towards Mercury with red and purple wings. She points her finger at Mercury. Hermes is trying to keep the peace.

> ROBIN: Because you shared my hateful **mother**'s bed? For how long? We are supposed to be friends!
> HERMES: Robin, please--

*Panel six*
Close up of Robin as she turns to Hermes who is looking devastated by this whole thing. This is not how the day was supposed to go, and now the woman he loves feels betrayed.

> ROBIN: And **you**! What were **you** here for, all this time?
> HERMES: I... it's not...

ROBIN: *"Tricks, but never lies."* We made a **pact**!
MERCURY [off panel]: Robin, heed--

## Page 14 – six panels

*Panel one*
Big, dramatic panel. Robin strikes Mercury across the face.

ROBIN: How **dare** you?!

*Panel two*
Mercury looks shocked and saddened at all of this, slightly holding his face where Robin struck him.

MERCURY: Robin, I'm... I'm sorry...

*Panel three*
Robin has turned away from them, on her knees, holding her face in her hands. Hermes is walking towards her, but Mercury has stopped him. Behind them, a portal is sparking up.

HERMES: Robin... I need to tell--
MERCURY: Brother, we **must** leave.

*Panel four*
Mercury is now pulling his brother into the portal.

HERMES: But-- I-- Robin, I--
MERCURY:[overlapping] I am truly sorry, Robin.

*Panel five*
Mercury now, in the portal as it's closing. He looks sincere and reticent.

MERCURY: For everything.

*Panel six*
Long shot of Robin, on her knees, head bowed and only Greenie looming above her. Robin's wings are deep blue in this solemn scene.

NO DIALOGUE

## Page 15 – six panels

*Panel one*
Same as last panel from previous page. Robin's head is now raised, we see tears have streamed from her eyes.

GREENIE [hollow]: Robin?
ROBIN [small]: ...How, Greenie?
ROBIN [small]: How could I have not seen **any** of this?

*Panel two*
Close up of Greenie, as he tries to explain and offer small comfort in his eyes.

GREENIE [hollow]: Mayhaps thee did. But refused to acknowledge it. Such is the prerogative of any child.
GREENIE [hollow]: And in truth, war should cometh as little surprise to the denizens of Faerie. The skin of our domain hath long itched with conflict.

*Panel three to six*
These are shown in a storybook style, sketches and on a yellow style parchment, showing how things go badly between Titania and Oberon.

*three*
The king and queen in a throne room, arguing heatedly.

> GREENIE [hollow, caption]: "For centuries, king and queen has't been waging a war of indignities...

*four*
Oberon, seductively cradling the chin of a early 20s maiden with one hand, holding a strawberry. The maiden looks entranced.

> GREENIE [hollow, caption]: "...oft using the mortals as weapons.

*five*
Now in a dark room, a hooded Titania whispers in the ear of a royal French scribe from the 13th century (male, beard) who is writing on parchment with his eyes closed and sparkling with magic, as if in a dream. It's dark, and a candle barely lights the scene.

> GREENIE [hollow, caption]: "Perception is power. And sadly, mortals are not the only ones capable of extreme vindictiveness...

*six*
We get closer to the scribe and see he's drawing Oberon a bit like in his original description from French medieval poetry - barely three feet high, dwarfish and somewhat hunched, a far cry from how he's seen in this story. He's with a braying donkey. Alongside this image we see the writing going off panel: Alas, the king of the fairies was a cruel, dwarfish

> GREENIE [hollow, caption]: "...or pettiness."

**Page 16 – six panels**

*Panel one*
Still showing the storybook style, sketches and on a yellow style parchment, we see the king and queen sitting on their throne, addressing dozens of faerie citizens. Oberon casts a loving sidewards glance at his smiling queen, without turning his head.

> GREENIE [hollow, caption]: "It is unlikely either monarch truly hated the other in the beginning. Even with their... infidelities."

*Panel two*
A cradle, with Robin as a baby, lying in it, gurgling. Her little horns and wings (transparent) already evident. Titania reads her a story - the start of 'lies' being told. As we get closer to the bottom of this panel, it gets darker.

> GREENIE [hollow, caption]: "Your very existence is testament to that, Robin."
> ROBIN [caption]: "...Then this war is only the second time they have been honest with each other.
> ROBIN [caption, small] "And with me."

*Panel three*
Back to the 'present', now. Robin is standing, looking determined. She's wiping her eyes and her wings are a dark orange. Greenie is passive, very matter of fact.

> ROBIN: Look at what their realm of lies has wrought.

ROBIN: We must depart this insanity.
GREENIE [hollow]: We cannot leave. I cannot. My duty is to millions of magical seeds which has't rested hither, long 'fore the first fairy setteth foot on our grass. Who else can protect our land's history?

*Panel four*
Greenie, close up. again, very aware that there's nothing that can be done.

ROBIN [off panel]: You can't be burned by their folly. There must be a way.
GREENIE [hollow]: Attempting it would destroy me.

*Panel five*
Same as last panel. An old leaf falls in front of Greenie, catching his attention.

GREENIE [hollow]: But... Hm.
GREENIE [hollow]: Hold.

*Panel six*
Same as last panel, but Greenie's eyes are closed and now he is glowing with golden energy, magic.

ELDER SEED [too small to read, no tail]: ...That is but her only chance.
GREENIE [hollow]: No... thee cannot mean... but milady... would needeth to...
ELDER SEED [too small to read, no tail]: ...bleed. I understand your concern. She will nev'r be the same. But you must tell her.

## Page 17 – five panels

*Panel one*
Robin looks up at Greenie, who explains what's just happened.

GREENIE [hollow]: ...Robin.
GREENIE: One of the Elder seeds hath suggested there may be a... chance. For thee to leave without forced return. Forbidden blood magik. Very fusty, very powerful. There is no true lore for it.

*Panel two*
Robin looks concerned as she listens.

GREENIE [hollow, off panel]: However, you must sacrifice something **significant** of yourself. Only then can the magik be cast.
ROBIN: What about you?

*Panel three*
The two talk, Robin showing apprehension, Greenie being straight forward, knowing what needs to be done. Robin's wings are light, pale orange.

GREENIE [hollow]: Both king and queen wilt not risk losing me ov'r this.
ROBIN: But... you...
GREENIE [hollow]: Make haste, Robin. Every second you waste, thy mother's spell takes stronger hold and even thy sacrifice may fail.

*Panel four*
Robin considers this, worry etched over her face as she thinks...

    ROBIN: I...

*Panel five*
Same as last panel but Robin turns away, realising what she's saying.

    ROBIN [small]: ... my wings.

## Page 18 – five panels

*Panel one*
Greenie, but for the first time, he looks scared.

    GREENIE [hollow]: ...Robin... this magik... t'will be irreversible and extremely painful.
    GREENIE [hollow]: Art thee certain?

*Panel two*
Robin looks down, her eyes concealed by darkness, her wings a terrified dark mustard yellow - she barely, nervously, holds out her knife on her palms (with both arms outstretched), trembling.

    NO DIALOGUE

*Panel three*
The knife hovers in mid air, surrounded by a hand made of green, leafy looking and golden energy as Greenie's magic takes it.

    NO DIALOGUE

*Panel four*
Robin takes off her belt (which also drops the play she's been carrying all through the story) as she kneels to the ground, almost as if this was an execution, as Greenie talks. Dark scene.

    GREENIE [hollow]: ...I shall be sure to seal the wounds once the blood hath been shed.

*Panel five*
The knife, held by the magic hand, hovers above Robin's wings, ready to make the cut...

    NO DIALOGUE

## Page 19 – six panels

*Panel one*
Blood (red blue) splatters across on to the ground.

    ROBIN [off panel, screaming]: AAAHHIIIGGGHHH

*Panel two*
A close up of Robin, clutching the ground in agony, tears streaming down her face. We can't see the wings in shot, but slight drops of blood can be seen.

    ROBIN [screaming]: HGAAAHH AAAAGGHH

*Panel three*
More blood on the ground, with Robin's kneeling legs in shot, slightly flecked with blood. This shouldn't be too explicit, even though the blood isn't pure red.

ROBIN [off panel, screaming]: AIIIGHHH HGG GGHH

*Panel four*
Wide shot, as Robin on her knees, wings cut off (grey and lifeless), and she's slightly splattered with drops of blood. We're too far away to see much of the damage and the blood from this distance should be dark (if that works). Her belt and the play are in the blood, too.

ROBIN [weary, tired]: ...hghh... uhh... did... ahh... hhh...

*Panel five*
Close up of her face, bowed, as she still kneels. A light off panel shines on her.

ROBIN [weary, tired]: ...did...nn... ghh...it... w... wor--

*Panel six*
Same as last panel, but she looks up at the off panel light, a slight smile of hope on her sweating, agonised face. The magic has worked.

NO DIALOGUE

## Page 20 – five panels

*Panel one*
Robin stands up ragged and staggering, wings cut off and the wound cauterised. Her wings are on the ground, as the blood soaks into the grass, with her belt and the play.

ROBIN: ...where... where does it... lead?

*Panel two*
Greenie looks at her bleakly.

GREENIE [hollow]: I... I doth not know.

*Panel three*
Robin looks back at the top of the kingdom's towers, looming in the distance through the trees.

ROBIN [small]: Anywhere but here.

*Panel four*
Robin puts a tender hand on the main tree where Greenie resides, a last touch goodbye for sentiment. She smiles sadly.

GREENIE [hollow]: What will thee do?
ROBIN: Hopefully... something true.

*Panel five*
Robin starts to walk towards the portal, turning her head to say her last goodbyes.

ROBIN: Thank you. For never... for not being **them**. Any of them.
GREENIE: What should I sayeth to thy... the monarchs?

*Panel one*
Robin turns back to Greenie properly, slightly hesitant.

> ROBIN: I doubt they will care.
> ROBIN [sad, small]: They've granted me more words today than
> they have in decades.
> GREENIE: They will ask.

*Panel two*
Robin ponders this, looking up into the distance.

> NO DIALOGUE

*Panel three*
Same again, but with a sad (and very slight) smile.

> ROBIN: Tell them I finally did what they wanted.

*Panel four*
Panning style shot, of the grey, slightly bloodied wings - we'll move across
in the same scene in the next panel.

> ROBIN CAPTION: "Tell them...

*Panel five*
Across from the last shot now, we see part of the wings and the play's cover
(with the title), flecked with drops of blood. As a call back to *Magic of Myths
Season 1*, red flowers are starting to grow where the blood has fallen.

> ROBIN CAPTION: "...I finally flew."